for Matilda
with wishes
♡
Emma
x

hello!

For Lili and Kitty Clifton
with love, Mummy x

With special thanks to Auntie Janet,
whose knitting skills made Pickle real,
and Auntie Valerie, who made sure.

ORCHARD BOOKS
338 Euston Road, London NW1 3BH
Orchard Books Australia
Hachette Children's Books
Level 17/207 Kent Street, Sydney, NSW 2000
First published in Great Britain in 2006
ISBN 1 84362 928 3
13 digit ISBN 9781843629283
Little Pickle Panda character © Emma Thomson 2004
A Night-time Adventure © Emma Thomson 2006
The right of Emma Thomson to be identified as the author and illustrator of this work
has been asserted by her in accordance with the Copyright, Designs and Patents Act, 1988.
A CIP catalogue record for this book is available from the British Library.
1 3 5 7 9 10 8 6 4 2
Printed in China

EMMA THOMSON'S
LILI
and
Pickle

A Night-time Adventure

Emma Thomson

ORCHARD BOOKS

Lili the ragdoll lived on the dresser in the kitchen. It was full of bits and bobs and good things to eat.

From the dresser, Lili could see everything that went on in the kitchen, but sometimes she was lonely and wished she had a best friend to share her home. Then, one moonlit night, someone new arrived ...

It was a little panda, curled up in a big bag of wool. He was trying to sleep, but he couldn't because he was in a strange place.

He felt frightened and lost, and he started to cry — Boo hoo! Boo hoo! — great big sobs for something so tiny, and big enough to wake Lili.

"Little panda," Lili asked kindly, "whatever is the matter?"

"I don't know how I got here," the panda sobbed. "I don't even know my name!"

"Look," said Lili, "your name is written on your label — Pickle. I shall call you Little Pickle Panda — because your name is Pickle and you're a little panda — and Pickle for short . . ."

"...And I think I can help you find out how you came to be in the kitchen," Lili continued, "but we'll have to go on a journey away from the dresser. It could be dangerous..."

Pickle didn't know if he was brave enough for an adventure – but with his new friend, Lili, by his side, he knew he had to try.

Very carefully, the two friends climbed down from the dresser. As they tiptoed across the kitchen floor, a huge monster appeared!

"I'll save you!" cried Pickle, and he quickly pulled Lili to safety until the monster had gone.

Next, they had to get past Archie Dog without waking him up. Lili was scared of Archie Dog.

"Don't worry," said Pickle, and he grabbed hold of a ribbon and they swung all the way above Archie's head ... wheeee!

They landed with a thud, right by the kitchen table.

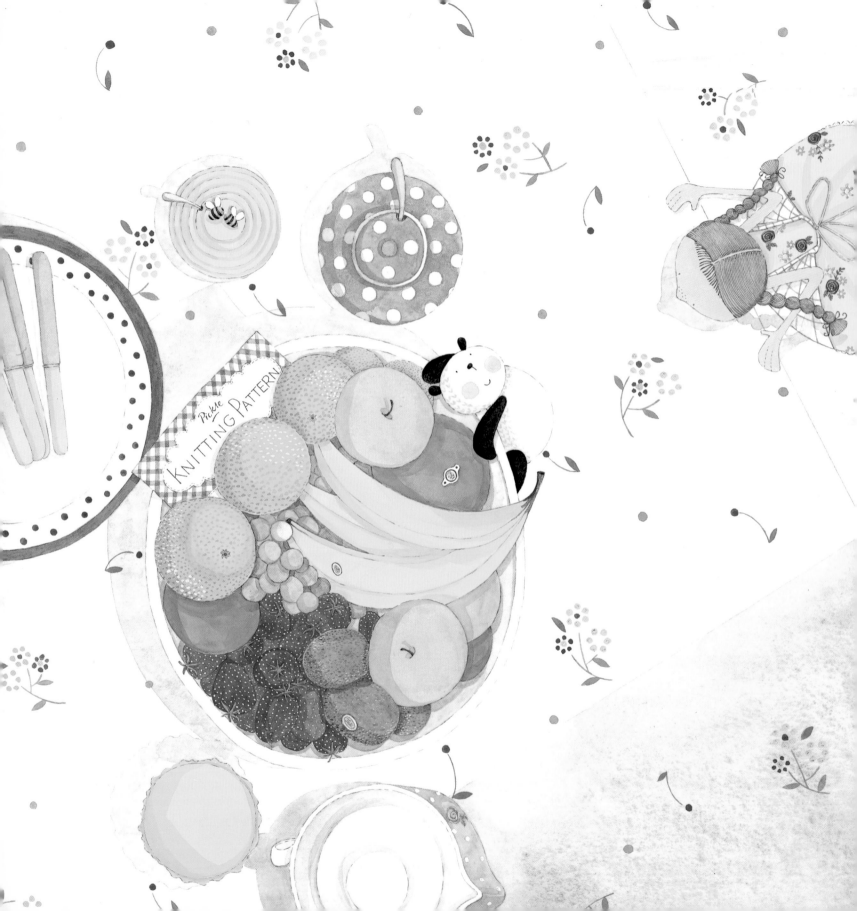

KNITTING PATTERN

Pickle

"The answer to how you came to the kitchen is up there," said Lili, pointing to the table top.
So Pickle climbed up.

He found jam and honey, strawberries, bananas and apples.

And then he found a knitting pattern. On the front were lots of pictures of little pandas just like him, dancing, singing and jumping! Pickle looked inside.

"Somebody knitted you from wool," Lili explained. "I think I know why."

"Why?" asked Pickle.

"Everyone needs a special best friend," said Lili, "and you were made to be my friend and live on the dresser with me."

"And will you be
my friend?" asked
Pickle, nervously.

"Oh, yes please!" smiled Lili.
"You saved me from the
scary monster . . .

. . . and made me brave enough
to swing past Archie Dog.

You were knitted
with love that shines
as brightly as
tonight's stars . . ."

" . . . and that means we'll be best friends forever!" laughed Lili, picking Pickle up and swirling him round in a big, happy swish.

Pickle didn't feel sad any more. His heart was bursting with happiness, just like the morning sun that had suddenly burst through the kitchen window and turned night into day.

It was time for Lili and Pickle to go home to the dresser. But the two friends knew they would have plenty more adventures together to come . . .

KNITTING PATTERN

Can you knit? Do you know someone who likes to knit? Why not ask them to knit you your very own Pickle? Make sure you give him lots of love!

ONE SIZE

KNIT WITH LOVE ♥

Silly

Sweet

funny

kind

Pickle

2.75mm needles
1 ball each of black & white 4 ply mercerised cotton
Work in stocking stitch throughout

BODY

Cast on 14 sts in white		
Row 1	Inc once in each st	(28 sts)
Row 2	Purl	(28 sts)
Row 3	Inc once in every other st	(42 sts)
St st for 3.5cm		
New Row	K4, K2tog, K9, Sl1 K1 psso, K8, K2tog, K9, Sl1 K1 psso, K4	(38 sts)
Next Row	Purl	(38 sts)
New Row	K4, K2tog, K7, Sl1 K1 psso, K8, K2tog, K7, Sl1 K1 psso, K4	(34 sts)
Next Row	Purl	(34 sts)
New Row	K4, K2tog, K5, Sl1 K1 psso, K8, K2tog, K5, Sl1 K1 psso, K4	(30 sts)
Next Row	Purl	(30 sts)
New Row	K4, K2tog, K3, Sl1 K1 psso, K8, K2tog, K3, Sl1 K1 psso, K4	(26 sts)
Next Row	Purl	(26 sts)
New Row	K4, K2tog, K1, Sl1 K1 psso, K8, K2tog, K1, Sl1 K1 psso, K4	(22 sts)
Next Row	Purl	(22 sts)
New Row	K4, K2tog, Sl1 K1 psso, K6, K2tog, Sl1 K1 psso, K4	(18 sts)
Next Row	Purl	(18 sts)
Next Row	K3, K2tog, Sl1 K1 psso, K4, K2tog, Sl1 K1 psso, K3	(14 sts)
Next Row	Purl	(14 sts)
New Row	K2tog K1 – to last 2 sts, K2tog	(9 sts)
Next Row	Purl	(9 sts)
Next Row	Cast off	

LEGS

Cast on 7 sts in black		(9 sts)
Row 1	Inc each end row	(11 sts)
Row 2	Inc each end row	(13 sts)
Row 3	Inc each end row	(15 sts)
Row 4	Inc each end row	
Row 5	Inc once in first st, K5, Sl1, K2tog, psso, K5, inc once in last st	(15 sts)
Row 6	P6, Sl1, P2tog, psso, P6	(13 sts)
Row 7	K6, K2tog, K5	(12 sts)
Rows 8–20	St st	(12 sts)
Row 21	K2tog throughout	(6 sts)
Row 22	Purl	
Thread through loops and pull up		

EARS

Cast on 4 sts in black
Work 3 rows in St st
P2tog twice
K2tog
Fasten off

HEAD

Cast on 12 sts in white		(24 sts)
Row 1	Inc once in each st	(24 sts)
Row 2	Purl	(24 sts)
Rows 3–15	St st	(12 sts)
Row 16	P2tog to end	(6 sts)
Row 17	K2tog to end	
Thread through loops and pull up		

Sew on eyes, nose, mouth and cheeks using coloured wool

ARMS

Cast on 3 sts in black		(6 sts)
Row 1	Inc in each st	(12 sts)
Row 2	Inc in each st	(12 sts)
Row 3	Purl	(12 sts)
Rows 4–11	St st	(10 sts)
Row 12	Dec first at each end of row	(10 sts)
Row 13	Purl	(8 sts)
Row 14	Dec first at each end of row	(8 sts)
Row 15	Purl	(6 sts)
Row 16	Dec first at each end of row	(6 sts)
Row 17	Purl	(3 sts)
Row 18	K2tog all along row	(3 sts)
Row 19	Purl	
Thread through loops and pull up		

attach here
attach here
attach here
attach here
attach here
attach here
attach here

Sew up each section and fill with stuffing, making
sure they are soft and plump. Attach as shown.

Knit each stitch with love to ensure a good heart